S0-AHC-315

HEIDI HECKELBECK

Sunshine Magic

By Wanda Coven
Illustrated by Priscilla Burris

LITTLE SIMON
New York London Toronto Sydney New Delhi

This book is a work of fiction. Any references to historical events, real people, or real places are used fictitiously. Other names, characters, places, and events are products of the author's imagination, and any resemblance to actual events or places or persons, living or dead, is entirely coincidental.

LITTLE SIMON
An imprint of Simon & Schuster Children's Publishing Division
1230 Avenue of the Americas, New York, New York 10020
First Little Simon hardcover edition January 2023
Copyright © 2023 by Simon & Schuster, Inc.
Also available in a Little Simon paperback edition.
All rights reserved, including the right of reproduction in whole or in part in any form. LITTLE SIMON is a registered trademark of Simon & Schuster, Inc., and associated colophon is a trademark of Simon & Schuster, Inc. For information about special discounts for bulk purchases, please contact Simon & Schuster Special Sales at 1-866-506-1949 or business@simonandschuster.com.
The Simon & Schuster Speakers Bureau can bring authors to your live event. For more information or to book an event contact the Simon & Schuster Speakers Bureau at 1-866-248-3049 or visit our website at www.simonspeakers.com.
Designed by Chrisila Maida
Manufactured in the United States of America 1222 LAK
10 9 8 7 6 5 4 3 2 1
This title has been cataloged with the Library of Congress.
ISBN 9781665911320 (hc)
ISBN 9781665911313 (pbk)
ISBN 9781665911337 (ebook)

CONTENTS

FLOATING SHORTS

Heidi Heckelbeck started her day by daydreaming in bed.

I wish I knew another witch my age, she thought. *Then we could share magical secrets and cast spells together and . . .*

Scrape! Clump! Scrape!

The sound of dresser drawers opening jolted Heidi upright.

She watched as her dresser drawers opened *all by themselves*. Then her folded clothes swooshed out of her bedroom and into the hall.

"That's new," said Heidi.

She chased her clothes downstairs, where there was a full-blown tornado of outfits in the living room. Heidi fended off a pair of underwear with her arm.

"What's going on?" Heidi asked.

Heidi's aunt turned around as a pair of shorts landed in an open suitcase.

"I'm *magic packing*, silly!" announced Aunt Trudy. "Didn't your mom tell you?"

Mom poked her head in from the kitchen. "No, because I wanted it to be a surprise!"

"Well then, *surprise!*" said Aunt Trudy. "We're going to Castle Spell Cove. Your mom and I used to vacation there when we were your age."

With a snap, the clothes landed in the open suitcases. Then the packed luggage zipped itself shut and floated out the front door.

"Um, what if the neighbors see our flying suitcases?" Heidi asked.

Aunt Trudy waved her off. "Don't worry. I put a shimmer spell around the yard. Our secret is safe. Now go get dressed so we can hit the beach!"

Heidi ran up the stairs and nearly bumped into an egg-and-cheese biscuit floating in front of her.

"Don't forget your breakfast!" Mom called.

Heidi shook her head. *What's with all the magic today?*

Her little brother,
Henry Heckelbeck,
snagged the biscuit
in   midair   and
took a big bite.

"Don't you love magic?" he said. "It's so tasty!"

"That was MINE!" Heidi complained.

Then—*POOF!*— another breakfast sandwich appeared for Heidi.

Her little brother might be a breakfast stealer, but he was right about one thing.

Heidi *did* love magic.

Chapter 2

SAND-SATiONAL!

The Heckelbecks never used magic to travel because Dad loved to drive.

Luckily, Heidi loved looking out the window. They passed a farm with a peach orchard and horses. They also passed an old mill with a waterfall, and then a lake filled with boats.

Finally, Heidi spotted a sign that read CASTLE SPELL COVE: THE SECRET SEASIDE VILLAGE WHERE DREAMS COME TRUE.

The car bumped along cobblestone streets lined with little shops with magical names like the Sand Witch Shop, Coven Creamery, and Spellbinder's Books.

"I see
the water!"
Heidi shouted as she
rolled down the window and
breathed in the salty air.

Dad turned down a sandy lane and
parked in a driveway speckled with
broken seashells.

"We're here!" he announced.

The cottage had gray shingles, white trim, and a bright blue door. It was so cute!

Dad unlocked the front door as Heidi and Henry raced inside to explore every room and find the perfect place to stay. Heidi picked an upstairs bedroom with views of the ocean.

She thudded back down the wooden stairs and onto the porch with a hammock.

Heidi flung herself onto the hammock and said, "This is the life!"

"Oh, it gets even better," said Aunt Trudy. "Want to see the beach before dinner?"

"Do I ever!" Heidi cheered as she leaped back up.

Then the whole Heckelbeck family wandered down to a sandy path that led through the dunes.

Heidi and Henry kicked off their shoes and raced to the beach.

The first thing they saw was the ocean, but then something else caught their eye.

"Wow!" shouted Henry. "Check out that sand-sational sandcastle!"

"That's not a sandcastle," said Heidi. "It's a sand KINGDOM!"

"I'm going to get a closer look!" Henry said.

He sprinted wildly toward the sandcastle, and Heidi called out, "Be careful!"

But it was too late! Henry tripped,
and was going to crash into the castle.
Oh no! thought Heidi. *I can't watch!*

But then a gust of strong wind came out of nowhere and pushed her brother back up.

"Phew! That was close!" Henry said. "I guess I'm just lucky!"

Heidi agreed, but she felt a charge in the air. It was a sizzle she'd felt before. Something that felt like magic.

Chapter 3

A WELL-KEPT SECRET

Eeee! Today is our first full day at the beach! thought Heidi as she hopped out of bed, already dressed in her swimsuit and matching shorts.

A plate with scrambled eggs and a cinnamon roll greeted her at the kitchen table.

Henry had already cleaned his plate. Mom and Aunt Trudy were packing an old-fashioned picnic basket with sandwiches, pretzels, chocolate chip cookies, and grapes.

"*Beep! Beep!*" said Dad as he wheeled a cooler into the kitchen.

"Did you pack any NEW sodas?" asked Henry. Sodas were a specialty in the Heckelbeck household. Dad worked for a soda company called The FIZZ.

"Well, we have water," said Dad. "And my new Ice-Cream Sodas, like Orange Vanilla and Strawberry Cheesecake!"

"Yay!" cried Heidi and Henry at the same time. Then they cleared their plates and gathered beach toys, a cabana, and folding chairs. They loaded everything onto a beach wagon and set off for the beach.

As they set up their cabana and chairs on the beach, Heidi looked around. "There's hardly anybody here!"

"Castle Spell Cove is *never* crowded," said Mom, winking at Aunt Trudy. "It's a well-kept secret."

Aunt Trudy laughed. "I'd say it's *more* than a well-kept secret."

Heidi didn't know what her aunt meant, but before she could ask, Henry yelled out, "Hey! The sand kingdom from yesterday is GONE."

How could a massive sand kingdom just disappear? Heidi wondered.

Then she remembered feeling magic in the air. Was Castle Spell Cove a magical place?

Heidi couldn't wait to find out.

Chapter 4

FiNE AND SANDY

Heidi and Henry put on sunscreen, grabbed their boogie boards, and raced into the water.

"Whoa! It feels great! Like taking a bath!" Henry said.

Heidi felt her feet sink into the soft rippled sand as she waded deeper.

Then they both jumped on their boogie boards. It was time to ride!

Heidi and Henry caught waves and rode them back to shore again and again. After that, they tossed their boards on the beach and played Frisbee.

Henry caught the Frisbee every time—because Heidi was better at throwing. Henry's throws either went too high or curved away from Heidi.

Mom waved the kids to the cabana and called out, "Lunchtime!"

The kids plunked onto towel-lined beach chairs. Heidi dug through the ice in the cooler and pulled out a water. Henry grabbed a soda.

"Why does food taste better at the beach?" asked Heidi, biting into a sandwich.

Henry popped a grape into his mouth. "Because EVERYTHING'S better at the beach!"

The whole family agreed.

Heidi watched other people as she ate. A dog raced after his owner. Some older kids skimboarded across the shallow waves. Then Heidi saw a girl her age with dark hair and brown skin. She was building a sandcastle.

Did she build the sandcastle we saw last night? Heidi wondered.

Chapter 5

SEAS THE DAY!

Heidi was surprised when another little boy appeared by their cabana.

"Hey!" the boy said to Henry. "I'm Arjun Akhtar. Wanna play?"

"Sure!" said Henry.

"Cool!" said Arjun. "This game is called Spinning Circles! You run in

circles until you reach the water. Last one to fall down wins!"

Heidi watched as Henry and his new friend spun around like two spinning tops. She wasn't sure if she would *ever* understand little brothers. They were just plain weird sometimes.

"You should make a new friend too, Heidi," said Aunt Trudy, who happened to be looking at the girl building the sandcastle. "You never know what you might have in common."

"You're right," Heidi said as she wiped the sand from her legs and took a deep breath. "Okay, here goes nothing!"

Heidi marched across the warm sand and stood in front of the girl's sandcastle. The girl was cutting tiny squares of wet sand with a Popsicle stick. She didn't notice Heidi at first.

"Hey," Heidi began, "your sandcastle is amazing."

The girl squinted at Heidi and smiled. "Thanks! You know, the trick is to have the right tools."

"Got it," said Heidi as she kneeled next to her. "The right tool makes it cool!"

The girl laughed. "Hey, you're funny! My name is Sunita Akhtar, but everyone calls me Sunny."

Heidi sat on the back of her heels. "I'm Heidi Heckelbeck. Everyone calls me . . . Heidi. Or Heckelbeck. I think my little brother just met your little brother."

Sunny looked up and saw Arjun and Henry running in circles. "Yep. I hope your brother knows a spell to cure the dizzies."

Heidi didn't know what to say to that. So she asked, "Um, mind if I watch you build?"

"I have a better idea," Sunny said. "You want to help me?"

Heidi's face lit up. "I'd love to!"

Sunny cut more squares, and Heidi spaced them along the battlement.

They looked like jack-o'-lantern teeth. Sunny also showed Heidi how to make stairs with a wooden ruler. Then they filled the moat with buckets of water.

"Did you build the sand kingdom that was here yesterday?" Heidi asked. Sunny nodded. "I did!"

"Where'd it go?" Heidi asked. "It was so beautiful!"

Sunny shrugged. "I like to start fresh every day. It's more fun that way."

Heidi nodded and looked at her side of the sandcastle. The towers were crooked, and the stairs were slanted. "Hmm, I'm not as good as you," she admitted.

Sunny laughed. "Oh, that will be an easy fix."

Then Sunny looked toward the sun
and—*swoosh!*—the crooked towers
straightened, and the slanted stairs
leveled out. The now-perfect castle
shimmered in the sun.

"There, that's better," said Sunny with a smile. "Now . . . race you to the water!"

As Sunny ran off, Heidi's mouth fell open. *Another girl just used MAGIC!*

Chapter 6

I'M NOT DREAMING

Heidi splashed into the water after Sunny.

As they both floated, Heidi turned to her new friend. "Can I ask you a weird question?"

"Oh, I love weird questions!" said Sunny. "Go for it!"

"Hmm, there's no easy way to ask this," said Heidi. "Are you a . . . a witch?"

"Of course I am, silly!" said Sunny as she wiped her wet hair out of her face. "I thought everyone at Castle Spell Cove was a witch. Aren't you?"

Heidi blinked. She had *never* been asked if *she* was a witch before. It was such a surprise! Heidi suddenly felt like her whole life had been a wave that was growing and growing and growing through the ocean, and now she was about to crash on the shore.

"YUP!" Heidi shouted, finally letting her secret free.

"Cool!" said Sunny, splashing water at Heidi.

The two friends got into a splash battle until Sunny pointed to something in the water near Heidi.

"Oh, hold still," she said.

Heidi froze solid and cried, "What is it?!"

Sunny kept her eyes on the water. "Just a little critter. I'll take care of it."

With a wave of her hand, Sunny magically lifted a jellyfish into the air and gently placed it farther out into the sea.

"There," she said. "Now we won't bother the jellyfish, and the jellyfish won't bother us."

Heidi gasped. "Whoa! How did you DO that?"

"I used magic, duh!" Sunny said with a laugh. "I get my power from the sun. My mom calls it Sunshine Magic. You know about magic, right? I thought you said you were a WITCH!"

"*I am,*" Heidi said nervously, "but I can only do magic with my medallion and *Book of Spells.*"

Sunny splashed back in surprise. "You're kidding—right?"

Heidi blushed and shook her head. "Nope, that's the truth."

Sunny smiled warmly. "I'm sorry, I didn't mean to sound snooty. It's just that there's a whole world of magic beyond the *Book of Spells*."

Heidi's eyes grew wide. "There IS?"

Heidi never imagined using magic *without* her *Book of Spells*. Aunt Trudy did magic all the time without the book, but that was Aunt Trudy. She was a grown-up! Were there other kids who could do magic like this?

"Hey, Sunny, um, would you ever teach me how to move things, um, like you just did?" Heidi asked.

This time Sunny beamed. "Yes! Of course! I'd love to!"

Heidi squealed with joy and held out her arm. "Okay, but first you have to splash me again."

"Why?" asked Sunny.

"Because I just can't believe I have a *witch friend*!" Heidi whispered like it was secret. "And I want to make sure I'm not dreaming."

"Believe it, buddy!" Sunny cheered as she splashed Heidi with all her might.

BELLY-BUTTONING

Back on the beach, Sunny handed Heidi a butterfly kite and kept a daisy one for herself. The girls ran to a wide-open space on the warm sand.

Heidi held her hand in the air. "There's not enough wind. We'll never get these kites off the ground."

"We don't need wind, silly," Sunny said. "We're going to fly our kites with MAGIC. Now I'm going to focus my thoughts on the kite and direct it with my mind."

Sunny let her kite go. It lifted into the air as if a gust of wind had caught hold of it.

Next she let out the string and ran down the beach. Then she ran back to Heidi.

She held up her hand to give Heidi a high five and yelled, "Your turn!"

Heidi held her kite in the air. Then she focused all her thoughts on the kite and let it go. *Crash!* The kite fell onto the sand. Heidi frowned.

"Hey, nice try!" Sunny cheered. "Now keep going!"

So Heidi did. And every time she tried, her kite thwacked onto the ground.

"My kite must be afraid of heights," said Heidi. "It won't even flutter! Maybe I'm doing the spell wrong because my kite wants to dig deeper into the sand."

"Aw, kite-flying magic takes A LOT of practice," Sunny assured her. "Wanna try something else? How about collecting seashells?"

67

"Okay," said Heidi, and she dragged her kite back to their towels and grabbed a pail.

As they walked to the ocean, Heidi asked, "So, what's your favorite shell?"

"Scallop shells, like these!" said Sunny. Then she faced the water and lifted her arms in the air. A wave washed in two perfect scallop shells.

Heidi picked up an orange one. "It's so pretty!"

Sunny picked up a purple one. "Now you try! Just call the kind of shell you want from the sea with your mind."

Heidi placed her bucket on the sand. She looked out to sea and concentrated on scallop shells.

Again a wave folded onto the shore, but the only thing it left behind was a hermit crab.

The hermit crab shook its claws at her and scuttled back into the water.

Heidi called to the shells again *and* again, but it was no use. The shells stayed put.

"Don't worry," Sunny said. "You'll get the hang of it. Remember, YOU'RE A WITCH, so you have the power."

Heidi nodded. She still had to get used to the idea that she had powers beyond her spell book.

"Hey, you want to know a cool way to find shells WITHOUT magic?" Heidi asked.

"Sure!" said Sunny.

They walked to a part of the beach striped with thousands of tiny pebbles. Heidi lay on her stomach and leaned on her elbows.

"If you look closely in between the pebbles, you'll find teeny-tiny shells," she said.

Sunny lay down beside Heidi, and the girls sifted through the pebbles with their fingers.

Heidi found one and showed it to Sunny.

"It's so small!" cried Sunny.

The girls continued to search for tiny shells. *Plink! Plink! Plink!* They popped tiny periwinkle, coquina, cockle, and scallop shells into their pails.

"We should give this sport a name!" said Sunny.

Heidi shifted positions and wiped some pebbles from her stomach. "Let's call it belly-buttoning, because you have to lie on your belly to find the shells."

Sunny giggled and smiled. "I'm glad I met you, Heidi Heckelbeck."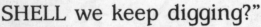

"Samesies!" said Heidi. "Now, SHELL we keep digging?"

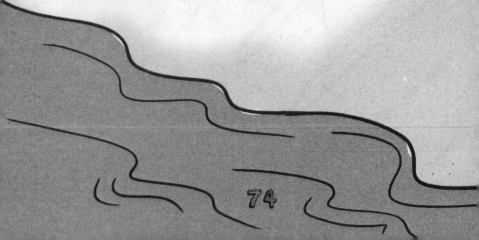

Chapter 8

PERFECTLY MAGICAL

The next morning, Sunny slapped a beach ball onto the surface of the water. The wind began to carry it out to sea.

"Okay, the beach ball is floating away," said Sunny. "I want you to use magic to bring it back."

Heidi looked worried. "I'll try."

Sunny narrowed her eyes. "This is NOT about trying, Heidi," she said. "It's about KNOWING and BELIEVING.

You have to know you have the power to bring that beach ball back."

Heidi clenched her fists. *You're a WITCH,* she told herself. *And you have the power to do this!*

But no matter how hard she tried, Heidi needed Sunny to bring the ball back.

"Okay, new plan," said Sunny. "Let's go to the pier."

The pier looked far away, but the walk was short and fun. Sunny told Heidi about where she lived, and Heidi told Sunny about her town, Brewster. They had a lot of things in common.

They both had little brothers. They both had two best friends. And most important, they were both magic!

As they walked onto the pier, Sunny pointed to the very end. "That's where we're going," she said.

The wind was blowing hard out, so far from the shore, and seagulls were flying happily.

"What are we doing out here?" Heidi asked when they reached the end of the pier.

Sunny pulled out two paper airplanes and handed one to Heidi. "We are going to fly these."

"In all this wind!" Heidi gulped. "I'll try, but—"

"Ahem," interrupted Sunny. "I'll have you know this is a no-'but' zone. So get flying! And remember, there's magic all around us at Castle Spell Cove."

Heidi and Sunny released their paper airplanes on the count of three. Sunny's stayed floating in the air, just like her kite yesterday, but Heidi's was carried off recklessly in the wild wind and snagged by a seagull.

"Merg," said Heidi.

But then the
seagull brought the
airplane back to
Heidi.

"See?" cheered
Sunny. "Magic is for the
birds, too! Don't give up!"

After playing a few more rounds of
paper airplane fetch with the seagull,
Heidi knew it wasn't going to happen.

"I have an idea," said Sunny. "Have
you ever heard of cornhole? It's not
magic, but it's a fun game!"

Heidi liked the sound of that, so
the girls ditched magic practice and

played beach games until the sun
went down.

Sunny and Heidi sat on the beach,
watching the giant pink clouds
in the sky.

"Pink clouds at night, sailors' delight," said Sunny. "What does that mean?" asked Heidi.

"Oh, it's an old sea rhyme," Sunny explained. "Pink clouds at sunset means we'll have good weather tomorrow."

"I hope so. It's our last full day here," said Heidi. "And maybe it's my last time to practice magic with you."

"Hey, just remember, there's always magic around you," said Sunny. "Check this out."

Sunny wiggled her fingers, and suddenly tiny lights started blinking on and off in the distance, like quiet fireworks on the beach.

Heidi gasped. "How did you do that?!"

"I didn't," Sunny confessed with a laugh. "It's not me. I'm not THAT good. But I know fireflies come out in the evening here. Aren't they cool?"

Heidi watched as the fireflies flickered in the night, and she agreed with her friend. "They're perfectly magical."

Chapter 9

LiFE'S A BEACH

Gray clouds raced across the sky at Castle Spell Cove. The waves crashed on the shore as Heidi walked along the beach.

"Can you believe this weather?" Sunny grumbled, walking up behind Heidi.

Heidi looked up at the sky. "Aw, I kind of LOVE cloudy days! Want to build a sandcastle?"

Sunny shrugged. "I guess so."

The girls kneeled on the beach and began to mound sand for the base. Sunny's side kept falling down.

"Ugh, why is the sand so crumbly today?" she complained, packing it back into place.

Heidi quietly scooped out the moat. Next, Sunny began to pat sand over her hand to make a drawbridge. But when she pulled her hand away, the drawbridge collapsed.

"Ugh, nothing's working today!" Sunny whined.

Heidi swished the palms of her hands back and forth to get the sand off. "Okay, then let's skip the castle and go for a swim."

The girls walked to the shore and dipped their toes in the water.

"*Brrr*, it's cold," said Sunny.

"It'll feel warm once we get in," Heidi said.

Then she dove into an oncoming wave.

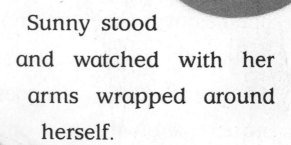

Sunny stood and watched with her arms wrapped around herself.

"No way. It's FREEZING!"

Heidi had to admit she was cold too. So the girls ran for their towels, and Heidi dried off. Then they zipped their hoodies over their bathing suits.

"Should we play magical metal detectors?" Sunny suggested. "We attract metal objects from the sand with magic!"

"Sounds magically magnetic!" cheered Heidi. "How does it work?"

"All you have to do is think like a metal detector," her friend said. "Watch!"

Sunny stared at the sand until—
zing!—a pull tab from a soda can shot
up from the beach.

"Ugh, just trash," Sunny said as
she shoved the pull tab in
her pocket to throw away
later.

Then she magically
unearthed a bobby pin,
a penny, and a bottle
cap.

"This is all JUNK,"
Sunny complained. "I hate
cloudy days. They block
out the sun and nothing
good ever happens. I'm going
home."

Heidi grabbed
her friend gently
by the arm.
"Wait! We both
leave tomorrow

morning, and I LOVE spending time with you. We don't need sunshine OR magic to have fun. I'll prove it!"

Then Heidi ran to her cabana and returned with two pails.

"We are going on an old-fashioned seashell hunt," said Heidi. "No magic allowed."

Sunny wrinkled her nose. "But, Heidi, we've already collected a gazillion tiny shells."

"We are only looking for big game this time," Heidi said firmly, setting off on the hunt.

Sunny halfheartedly followed.

"See, when the ocean is really wild on overcast days like these, that's the best time to look for shells," Heidi explained.

Sure enough, the shore was filled with giant seashells!

"WOW, I've never seen so many shells in my life!" Sunny exclaimed. "Even at the beach stores in town!"

Then the girls combed the beach and found shells with soft pinks, cool blues, pearly whites, and sunset oranges! They found long, colorful shells that looked like designer fingernails!

Heidi even found a full-size whelk shell. She held it up to her ear and could hear the ocean!

But then Sunny made the best discovery of all.

"Hey! It's a WHOLE sand dollar!"

Sunny cried. "All in one piece and not broken! Come look!"

Heidi inspected the round sand dollar. It had been bleached white from the sun and had a beautiful star flower in the center.

"These are rare!" Heidi told her. "Now aren't you glad you didn't go home?"

Sunny nodded. "So glad. And sorry for being such a grump earlier. You've been the magical one today."

"That's what friends are supposed to be!" Heidi cheered. "Wait, if you have Sunshine Magic, is there such a thing as Friend Magic?"

"Hmm, maybe?" said Sunny. "I don't know EVERYTHING about magic. I mean, that's why I'll go to Broomsfield Academy for middle school. That's where they teach kids like us."

"Broomsfield Academy? Never heard of it," said Heidi. "But I'm happy in Brewster, even if I'm the only kid like me there."

Sunny put her sand dollar away.

"Well, there IS a last-day tradition
at Castle Spell Cove . . . and it involves
ice cream," said Sunny with a smile.
"Are you interested?"

"Sign me up!" said Heidi.

Chapter 10

SEA YOU LATER!

The curtains beside Heidi's bed swished in the gentle sea breeze.

I can't believe we LEAVE today, she thought. *It's been the BEST vacation I've ever had.*

Suddenly a package magically flew through Heidi's open window!

There was a note on top with *To Heidi* written in swirly letters. Heidi read the note first.

Hey, Heidi!!

Had to leave early this morning, but thanks for the BEST week ever. Wish we went to the same school. Maybe someday we will! For now, would you like to be pen pals? Keep practicing your magical moves! Miss you already!

Love,
Sunny, your BWFF (Best Witch Friend Forever!!)

Next Heidi opened the box and pulled back the tissue paper. Sunny had made a beautiful sign with the itty-bitty seashells she had found. The shells were mounted on a piece of driftwood and said one word: *Believe*.

A magical warmth washed over Heidi, and she realized something on a new level. *I'm a witch—a REAL witch, with my very own magical powers.* And for the first time in her life, Heidi truly believed it.

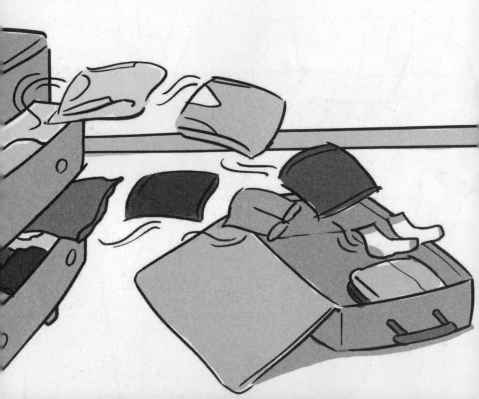

Magical powers or not, it was time to go, and Heidi still needed to pack her clothes. But as soon as she thought about packing, Heidi's clothes flew from the drawers and neatly packed themselves in her suitcase.

Heidi squealed. "I DID it!"

Then Aunt Trudy opened the door.

"Good! You're packed and ready to roll!"

Heidi's heart sank a little, because she thought she'd done the magic herself. But it was clearly her aunt's doing again.

"Thanks, Aunt Trudy," said Heidi.

"For what?" Aunt Trudy asked.

"You know, the magic packing," Heidi said, pointing to her suitcase.

"Oh, dear, that wasn't me," said Aunt Trudy. "I've had my magic hands full with cleaning the rest of the house. Now get a move on! We need to hit the road to beat the traffic."

Heidi clasped her hands together. *So it WAS me!* she thought . . . and she couldn't wait to tell Sunny!

"Hey, Sis," said Henry from the doorway. "Dad needs your suitcase."

Wow, Heidi had almost completely forgotten her little brother was even at the beach. But even Henry couldn't bother her today.

"On my way," she said.

In the driveway Heidi watched the others leaving Castle Spell Cove.

Car after car drove by, filled with happy, magic families that Heidi didn't know. Until one car drove past with a girl staring out the window who was the last person Heidi expected to see.

"Was that Melanie Maplethorpe?" Heidi asked.

Henry looked, but the car was gone. "No," he said. "What would SHE be doing at Castle Spell Cove?"

But what if it WAS Melanie? Heidi tried to dismiss this highly unpleasant thought. *Because there is absolutely NO WAY Melanie Maplethorpe, Heidi's number one enemy from Brewster, could possibly be here* . . . in a magical place for witches.

There's more

HE★D★ HECKELBECK

to explore!

LOOKING FOR MORE MAGIC? TRY

Jeanie & Genie